Dog Lies

by Bob McGrath

Illustrated by Meredith Johnson

PRICE STERN SLOAN

Los Angeles

For his continued good advice, and for taking the time to read and evaluate each story in the Bob's Books series, I would like to thank Dr. Gerald S. Lesser, Professor of Education and Developmental Psychology, Harvard University; Chairman, Board of Advisors, The Children's Television Workshop.

For their sensitive and encouraging input, I would also like to thank the following:

Julia Cummins, Coordinator of Children's Services of the New York Public Library

Dr. Richard Graham, Former Director of the Center for Moral Education and Development at Harvard University

Tom Greening, Ph.D., Editor of the Journal of Humanistic Psychology

Betty Long, Senior Children's Librarian, General Library of the Performing Arts at Lincoln Center (New York Public Library)

Valeria Lovelace, Director of Research - "Sesame Street"

Ann Sperry McGrath, children's book author and preschool teacher

Hannah Nuba, Director of the New York Public Library Early Childhood Resource and Information Center

Lisa Ann Marsoli, Editorial Director — Juvenile Division, Price Stern Sloan

Copyright © 1989 by Bob McGrath
Published by Price Stern Sloan, Inc.
360 North La Cienega Boulevard, Los Angeles, California 90048

ISBN: 0-8431-2396-6
Library Of Congress Catalog Card Number: 89-30678
10 9 8 7 6 5 4 3 2 1

"Josephine, did you feed Shag yet?" Jo's mom hollered from upstairs. It was the third time she had asked Jo to feed her dog. "Aunt Helen and Uncle John just drove up and I want that dog to behave!"

Jo had a choice. She could go and feed Shag now or she could go to the door to see if her favorite aunt and uncle had brought her a present. They always knew exactly what she liked. Jo decided to tell a little white lie. "Yes, Mom, I did," she said as she ran to the front door.

I'll feed Shag in a few minutes, she thought to herself. But as soon as her aunt and uncle handed Jo her surprise, she forgot all about feeding Shag.

Jo brought them into the living room, sat them down and opened the present. It was a new styrofoam glider plane with a two-foot wingspan. She had seen one in a department store a couple of weeks before and had really wanted to try it.

Her uncle said, "Let's go out in the backyard, put it together and see how it flies."

They were just getting the wings on when Jo's mother called from the kitchen. "Jo, your dog's being a brat and bothering Aunt Helen. Come in and get him."

Jo ran into the kitchen. "I'll be right back Uncle John," she said. But when she got to the kitchen, Shag began to run in circles, begging to be fed.

"Why is he acting that way?" her mother asked her. "He never acts like that with a full stomach. This dog's behavior is getting worse and worse."

"Maybe he just needs a little more to eat," Jo mumbled.

"Josephine," her mother said, "you know how many times I've told you not to overfeed that dog. He's in good shape right now. No more food."

Jo knew she was really in a jam. She had told her mother that she had already fed Shag and she didn't want her to find out she had lied, especially in front of her favorite aunt. She thought to herself, Wow, how do I get myself out of this one? Maybe I'll just take him out to the backyard.

Jo grabbed Shag by the collar and took him outside.

"What's wrong with your dog, Jo? He's really acting funny," her uncle asked.

Jo had a choice. She could tell her uncle that she had lied about feeding Shag, or she could tell him that she didn't know why the dog was acting funny. She decided it would be easier not to tell him about the lie.

"Oh, I don't know, maybe he's just excited. He gets excited when people come to the house," she said, and realized that she had just told another lie.

"Well, we can't fly the plane with him running around like that," her uncle said, going back into the house. "He might run after it and break it."

Jo sat alone on the back steps and thought to herself, Why did I ever tell Mom that I had fed Shag? That was a big mistake. I better go and tell her what I did right now. But by the time Jo entered the kitchen, her mother was busy cooking, talking to everyone and setting the table.

Just as she was about to tell her the truth, she realized how busy her mother was. I better not interrupt her right now, Jo thought, I'll tell her later.

Jo was in trouble. Her dog needed food, but there was no way she could get it out of the kitchen without everyone seeing her. She went back outside to decide what to do. Then she looked next door and saw her neighbor, Mr. Zimmerman. I know, she thought, I'll ask him for some dog food and feed Shag in the garage. That way Mom will never know and Shag will be happy.

"Mr. Zimmerman! Mr. Zimmerman!" Jo yelled, running to the fence. "Do you have some extra dog food I can borrow?"

Mr. Zimmerman smiled at Jo as he walked over to her. "Got a hungry dog that ate up all his food, young lady?"

"Uh huh," Jo mumbled, and thought to herself,
There goes another lie.

"I don't know, I might have a couple of cans for
you. I'll take a look and give you a call at your
house," Mr. Zimmerman said.

Jo thought to herself, Oh my gosh, what if he calls and Mom answers the phone? She said, "You don't have to call. I'll come over with you and take a look."

"No, don't bother, Jo. I might have to check in the basement. I'll go in and take a look and give you a call in a few minutes."

Jo got a sinking feeling in her stomach and thought, Now what do I do? I better make sure I answer the phone before anyone else does, or they'll want to know why I asked Mr. Zimmerman for dog food. She knew she couldn't bring Shag into the house with her to wait for the phone call, so she put him into the garage and shut the door.

Then she ran as fast as she could to get to the upstairs phone in her mother and father's room, where no one would hear her talking about dog food.

Jo sat next to the phone, hoping it would ring. Her heart was pounding. She thought, Wow, I'm really in a mess. I never thought that telling one little lie to Mom would turn into telling a million more lies.

It seemed like forever until Mr. Zimmerman called. Finally the phone rang and she grabbed the receiver as fast as she could. Thank goodness no one else answered it.

"Hello?" Jo said.

"Hi Jo," Mr. Zimmerman said. "I guess we both have hungry puppies today. I'm fresh out of dog food. Sorry."

Jo thought, Oh no, but managed a faint, "Thank you. That's OK," and hung up.

Now what would she do? How would she be able to feed Shag without her mother finding out? Jo decided that she would ask her sister to go to the store with her. If Nicole was in a good mood, she might say yes.

Nicole was carrying chairs into the dining room when Jo found her. Jo tapped her on the back and whispered, "Can you take me to the store for a minute?"

"What for, Jo? We're almost ready to eat," her sister said.

Jo thought fast, "We're out of chocolate ice cream."

"But Jo, we're having vanilla ice cream with raspberry sauce."

"But you know I like chocolate."

Nicole thought about it for a moment. "Well, Uncle John likes it too, so if we hurry I guess we'll have time to get some before we eat."

"Thanks, Nicole, you're the best," Jo said, giving a sigh of relief. She thought that at last she had solved all her problems. Once they were at the store she knew she could buy some dog food. She ran upstairs to get money from her bank.

Nicole was waiting by the car when Jo got back, but just as they were about to get in, Jo realized that something was wrong. Shag usually barked like mad when he was left in the garage, but now he wasn't making a sound.

She said, "Wait a minute, Nicole," and ran to see if Shag was all right. Then Jo panicked. The door was open and Shag was gone. Oh no, she thought, What else can happen today? She ran back to the car, almost ready to cry. "Nicole! Shag is missing! I put him in the garage and he got out. We have to find him!"

"This isn't the right time for that dog to be missing. Mom will be upset if we're late for dinner," Nicole said. But when she looked at Jo's face, she knew she had to help her. "OK. Hop in the car, we'll go around the block and look for him. Don't worry, we'll find him."

They circled their own block first and didn't find him. Then as they went in the direction of the market, they saw a police car with its lights flashing. Jo took a closer look and yelled, "Nicole, you better stop. Look over there!"

What they saw was a very serious-looking policeman holding a chicken by one wing and a very angry old lady. They also saw a shopping cart tipped over on its side with groceries around it. But worst of all, they saw Jo's hungry dog barking at the chicken and licking his chops.

Nicole just sighed and said, "Josephine, he's your dog. You take care of it."

Jo didn't want to get out of the car. She didn't want to face the policeman or the lady. She said to herself, Why didn't I feed Shag when I said I did? Why did I lie to Mom? She took a deep breath, got out of the car, and went over to her dog. "Oh, hi boy!" she said with a big phony smile.

"Is this your dog, Miss? I was just about to look up his tag number and call the dog warden," the policeman said in a firm voice.

Jo was too embarrassed to answer.

The lady shook her finger at her. "Don't you ever feed your dog? When I came out of the store he knocked my cart over and tried to steal my chicken!"

Jo still couldn't talk, but she thought to herself, I'll never do this again.

Finally, the policeman noticed her sister in the car and told Jo to take the dog home and tie him up. Jo grabbed Shag and put him in the car as fast as she could.

Nicole turned to her and said, "Forget the ice cream. Dinner is probably on the table by now. We're going straight home, and as soon as we get there, I'm telling Mom what happened."

Jo thought to herself, This is it. I'll have to tell the truth now. Mom will be upset and everyone will know that I lied. But when they got home, dinner was on the table, and before Jo could do a thing, Shag raced into the dining room and began barking and begging for food.

Jo's mother listened to Nicole's story, looked at Jo's father and then at Jo. She said in a determined voice, "This is your dog and you'll have to take care of him while we're eating. Please keep him quiet, and out of our way. I'll fix you a big plate of food. Where would you like to eat it?"

Jo breathed a sigh of relief. She wasn't going to have to tell her mother that she had lied to her, at least not yet. So she said, "We'll go up to my room."

Jo's mother fixed her a heaping dish of turkey, stuffing, mashed potatoes—the works, and Jo carried it up to her room with Shag close behind her. She wasn't upset about eating dinner upstairs, or even about missing dinner with the family, because she hadn't gotten caught.
Once Shag was safely in her room, she figured she could sneak down while everyone was eating and finally get some dog food.

Everything was going smoothly on her trip to the kitchen, until she was just about to open a can of dog food. At that moment her mother came into the kitchen to refill the gravy boat. "What are you doing with that dog food?" she asked.

"Well, I'm taking some up to Shag," Jo stammered. "You know I don't like to eat alone."

Jo's mother laughed, "No, Jo, put that can back. It's really a waste of food. He just ate a little while ago. You don't want to spoil him."

Just as she was about to go back to the dining room with the gravy, Jo said, "Hold it, Mom, I think I better tell you something."

"What's that, dear?" she said.

"I didn't really feed the dog," she said. "I was in a big hurry to see what Uncle John and Aunt Helen had brought me."

"I thought you said that you had." Her mother looked puzzled.

"I'm sorry," she said, "it was a lie, wasn't it?"

"You mean that's why Shag has been acting so crazy all evening?" her mother said.

"Yup," Jo answered.

"That poor dog! Please take some food up to him right now. How could you treat him this way? And I thought he was misbehaving," she sighed. "We'll talk about your part in all of this later."

Jo looked at her mother and said, "I'm sorry, Mom. Believe me, this will never happen again." And she trudged back upstairs.

She thought to herself, Thank goodness this lie is over. I was getting sick of it. I'll never, never, never tell another lie.